TERRIBLE TIMES TABLES

For Sascha, with love.
—M.M.

To my little Oliver, who is learning
his terrible times tables. —M.L.

Text copyright © 2019 Michelle Markel
Illustrations copyright © 2019 Merrilee Liddiard
Book design by Melissa Nelson Greenberg

Library of Congress Cataloging-in-Publication Data available.

ISBN: 978-1-944903-75-6
Printed in China.
10 9 8 7 6 5 4 3 2 1

Cameron Kids is an imprint of Cameron + Company

Cameron + Company
Petaluma, CA 94952
www.cameronbooks.com

TERRIBLE TIMES TABLES

by Michelle Markel

art by Merrilee Liddiard

cameron kids

TERRIBLE TABLE OF CONTENTS

5×1=5 5×2=10 5×3=15 5×4=20 5×5=25 5×6=30 5×7=35

BACK TO SCHOOL

2×1=2 2×2=4 2×3=6 2×4=8 2×5=10 2×6=12 2×7=14 2×8=16

3×1=3 3×2=6 3×3=9 3×4=12 3×5=15 3×6=18 3×7=21 3×8=24

4×1=4 4×2=8 4×3=12 4×4=16 4×5=20 4×6=24 4×7=28

2

2 x 1 is 2

We're stuck with you-know-who.

2 x 2 is 4

New kids are at the door.

2 x 3 is 6

They're up to their old tricks.

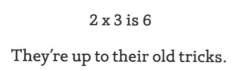

2 x 4 is 8

Please! I cannot wait.

2 x 5 is 10

Kevin broke his pen.

2 x 6 is 12

What's crawling on that shelf?

2 x 7 is 14

Cecelia's turning green.

2 x 8 is 16

Ick. A moldy tangerine.

2 x 9 is 18

I sail off into a dream.

5×1=5 5×2=10 5×3=15 5×4=20 5×5=25 5×6=30 5×7=35

2×1=2 2×2=4 2×3=6 2×4=8 2×5=10 2×6=12 2×7=14 2×8=16

3×8=24 3×7=21 3×6=18 3×5=15 3×4=12 3×3=9 3×2=6 3×1=3

HALLOWEEN

4×1=4 4×2=8 4×3=12 4×4=16 4×5=20 4×6=24 4×7=28

3

3 x 1 is 3

What are you going to be?

3 x 2 is 6

The principal's a witch.

3 x 3 is 9

Ve vant to get in line.

3 x 4 is 12

Let out your wild selves.

3 x 5 is 15

Your jack-o'-lantern's mean.

3 x 6 is 18

The storm blew in on Halloween.

3 x 7 is 21

A haunted house! You better run.

3 x 8 is 24

I dropped an eyeball on the floor.

3 x 9 is 27

No one scares me more than Kevin.

5×1=5 5×2=10 5×3=15 5×4=20 5×5=25 5×6=30 5×7=35

2×1=2 2×2=4 2×3=6 2×4=8 2×5=10 2×6=12 2×7=14 2×8=16

3×1=3 3×2=6 3×3=9 3×4=12 3×5=15 3×6=18 3×7=21 3×8=24

FIELD TRIP

4×1=4 4×2=8 4×3=12 4×4=16 4×5=20 4×6=24 4×7=28

4

4 x 1 is 4

Sam pukes. Sam pukes some more.

4 x 2 is 8

You're half an hour late.

4 x 3 is 12

Step back!
You'll hurt yourselves.

4 x 4 is 16

Welcome to the Pleistocene.

4 x 5 is 20

Skeletons. So many!

4 x 6 is 24

Bella rode a dinosaur.

4 x 7 is 28

Pick up a knife. Decapitate.

4 x 8 is 32

Oops. I thought these insects flew.

4 x 9 is 36

Kevin stole my trail mix.

Top border: $5 \times 1 = 5$ $5 \times 2 = 10$ $5 \times 3 = 15$ $5 \times 4 = 20$ $5 \times 5 = 25$ $5 \times 6 = 30$ $5 \times 7 = 35$

Left border: $2 \times 1 = 2$ $2 \times 2 = 4$ $2 \times 3 = 6$ $2 \times 4 = 8$ $2 \times 5 = 10$ $2 \times 6 = 12$ $2 \times 7 = 14$ $2 \times 8 = 16$

Right border: $3 \times 8 = 24$ $3 \times 7 = 21$ $3 \times 6 = 18$ $3 \times 5 = 15$ $3 \times 4 = 12$ $3 \times 3 = 9$ $3 \times 2 = 6$ $3 \times 1 = 3$

LUNCHTIME

Bottom border: $4 \times 1 = 4$ $4 \times 2 = 8$ $4 \times 3 = 12$ $4 \times 4 = 16$ $4 \times 5 = 20$ $4 \times 6 = 24$ $4 \times 7 = 28$

5

5 x 1 is 5

A roach—and it's alive!

5 x 2 is 10

Mystery meat again.

5 x 3 is 15

My nose has grown a bean.

5 x 4 is 20

Don't worry kids, there's plenty.

5 x 5 is 25

Never look her in the eye.

5 x 6 is 30

My retainer's dirty.

5 x 7 is 35

Someone's throwing plastic knives.

5 x 8 is 40

Have a nice lunch, Shorty!

5 x 9 is 45

Bella choked, but she'll survive.

5×1=5 5×2=10 5×3=15 5×4=20 5×5=25 5×6=30 5×7=35

2×1=2 2×2=4 2×3=6 2×4=8 2×5=10 2×6=12 2×7=14 2×8=16

3×1=3 3×2=6 3×3=9 3×4=12 3×5=15 3×6=18 3×7=21 3×8=24

WINTER PAGEANT

4×1=4 4×2=8 4×3=12 4×4=16 4×5=20 4×6=24 4×7=28

6

6 x 1 is 6

Silly winter skits.

6 x 2 is 12

Calling all our elves!

6 x 3 is 18

I forgot I'm in this scene!

6 x 4 is 24

The babies cry. The parents snore.

6 x 5 is 30

These risers don't feel sturdy.

6 x 6 is 36

Cue the singing candlesticks.

6 x 7 is 42

Everybody's looking at you.

6 x 8 is 48

Bella met an awful fate.

6 x 9 is 54

Uh oh, Santa's pants just tore.

5×1=5 5×2=10 5×3=15 5×4=20 5×5=25 5×6=30 5×7=35

2×1=2
2×2=4
2×3=6
2×4=8
2×5=10
2×6=12
2×7=14
2×8=16

3×8=24
3×7=21
3×6=18
3×5=15
3×4=12
3×3=9
3×2=6
3×1=3

VALENTINE'S DAY

4×1=4 4×2=8 4×3=12 4×4=16 4×5=20 4×6=24 4×7=28

7

7 x 1 is 7

I'm getting sick of Kevin.

7 x 2 is 14

Who left this message on my screen?

7 x 3 is 21

The frosting melted in the sun.

7 x 4 is 28

We drew lovebugs on your plate.

7 x 5 is 35

Flowers gave the teacher hives.

7 x 6 is 42

Kissing is disgusting!
Eewwwww.

7 x 7 is 49

Nibbles chewed my Valentine.

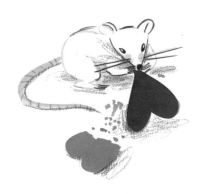

7 x 8 is 56

I brought a bag of candy lips.

7 x 9 is 63

Does Bella have a crush on me?

Top border: 5×1=5 5×2=10 5×3=15 5×4=20 5×5=25 5×6=30 5×7=35

Left border: 2×1=2 2×2=4 2×3=6 2×4=8 2×5=10 2×6=12 2×7=14 2×8=16

Right border: 3×1=3 3×2=6 3×3=9 3×4=12 3×5=15 3×6=18 3×7=21 3×8=24

Bottom border: 4×1=4 4×2=8 4×3=12 4×4=16 4×5=20 4×6=24 4×7=28

ART CLASS

8 x 1 is 8

Ready, set, create!

8 x 2 is 16

Step into my time machine.

8 x 3 is 24

Knock it over, out it pours.

8 x 4 is 32

Someone painted Nibbles blue.

8 x 5 is 40

Every picture tells a story.

8 x 6 is 48

It looks like you! It came out great.

8 x 7 is 56

Some mistakes are hard to fix.

8 x 8 is 64

The artist's name is Salvador.

8 x 9 is 72

Kevin's got a new tattoo.

5×1=5 5×2=10 5×3=15 5×4=20 5×5=25 5×6=30 5×7=35

2×1=2 2×2=4 2×3=6 2×4=8 2×5=10 2×6=12 2×7=14 2×8=16

3×1=3 3×2=6 3×3=9 3×4=12 3×5=15 3×6=18 3×7=21 3×8=24

END OF THE YEAR

4×1=4 4×2=8 4×3=12 4×4=16 4×5=20 4×6=24 4×7=28

9

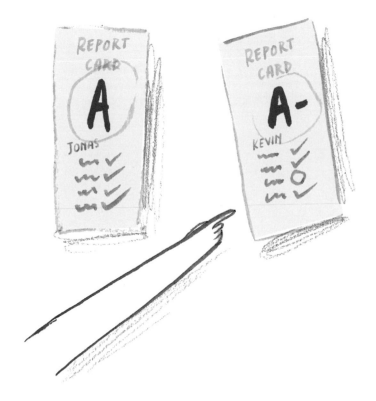

9 x 1 is 9

Your grades are worse than mine.

9 x 2 is 18

Scrub them 'til they're clean.

9 x 3 is 27

Only six more days of Kevin.

9 x 4 is 36

Ants invade the school picnic.

9 x 5 is 45

Bella found a buzzing hive.

9 x 6 is 54

We get to have a water war!

9 x 7 is 63

Too much sun for me.

9 x 8 is 72

I've never had a friend like you.

9 x 9 is 81

Good-bye Nibbles, it's been fun.

SCHOOL

10 x 1 is 10

We're outta here. The End!

MULTIPLICATION
✲ TABLES ✲

2

2 x 1 is 2
2 x 2 is 4
2 x 3 is 6
2 x 4 is 8
2 x 5 is 10
2 x 6 is 12
2 x 7 is 14
2 x 8 is 16
2 x 9 is 18

3

3 x 1 is 3
3 x 2 is 6
3 x 3 is 9
3 x 4 is 12
3 x 5 is 15
3 x 6 is 18
3 x 7 is 21
3 x 8 is 24
3 x 9 is 27

4

4 x 1 is 4
4 x 2 is 8
4 x 3 is 12
4 x 4 is 16
4 x 5 is 20
4 x 6 is 24
4 x 7 is 28
4 x 8 is 32
4 x 9 is 36

5

5 x 1 is 5
5 x 2 is 10
5 x 3 is 15
5 x 4 is 20
5 x 5 is 25
5 x 6 is 30
5 x 7 is 35
5 x 8 is 40
5 x 9 is 45

6

6 x 1 is 6
6 x 2 is 12
6 x 3 is 18
6 x 4 is 24
6 x 5 is 30
6 x 6 is 36
6 x 7 is 42
6 x 8 is 48
6 x 9 is 54

7

7 x 1 is 7
7 x 2 is 14
7 x 3 is 21
7 x 4 is 28
7 x 5 is 35
7 x 6 is 42
7 x 7 is 49
7 x 8 is 56
7 x 9 is 63

8

8 x 1 is 8
8 x 2 is 16
8 x 3 is 24
8 x 4 is 32
8 x 5 is 40
8 x 6 is 48
8 x 7 is 56
8 x 8 is 64
8 x 9 is 72

9

9 x 1 is 9
9 x 2 is 18
9 x 3 is 27
9 x 4 is 36
9 x 5 is 45
9 x 6 is 54
9 x 7 is 63
9 x 8 is 72
9 x 9 is 81

(10 x 1 is 10) . . .